MY MOTHER
SENDS HER WISDOM

BY LOUISE McCLENATHAN

ILLUSTRATED BY

ROSEKRANS HOFFMAN

William Morrow and Company   New York 1979

Library of Congress Cataloging in Publication Data

McClenathan, Louise.
My mother sends her wisdom.
Summary: A peasant woman uses her wisdom to outwit the local moneylender
    who is expecting to take over her farm.
I. Hoffman, Rosekrans. II. Title.   PZ7.D5574My   [E]   79-164
ISBN 0-688-22193-9   ISBN 0-688-32193-3 lib. bdg.

To Joe's mother, who grew up in old Russia
Louise McClenathan

For young Bob and old Bob and Miss Judy
Rosekrans Hoffman

"Mama," cried Katya, as she peered through the cottage window, "Old Boris, the moneylender, is coming down the road in his horse cart."

"Let him come, little one," answered Katya's mother, as she worked warm dough for bread. The dough made a soft slapping sound against the wooden table.

Boris and Alexei, the small boy who kept his accounts, drew up before the cottage, and the gentle sounds of the house were shattered by the old man's loud pounding on the door. "Widow Petrovna," he shouted, "I have come to collect your monthly rubles due me from the loan of silver to your late husband." His eyes were topaz yellow, like a cat's eyes, and his voice rasped with the sound of greed. Alexei stood with his ledger book and pen, waiting for the rubles to be dropped into his master's soft leather purse.

Mama stood behind Katya, slowly wiping her floury hands on her apron. "Tomorrow, Old Boris," she said, "I shall send you a fine fat goose and gander. My daughter will bring them to your house in the city. Today they would make a clamor in your cart, and the ride would upset the goose's laying. They will be my payment to you this month."

"Very well then, but no later than sundown tomorrow," Boris said.

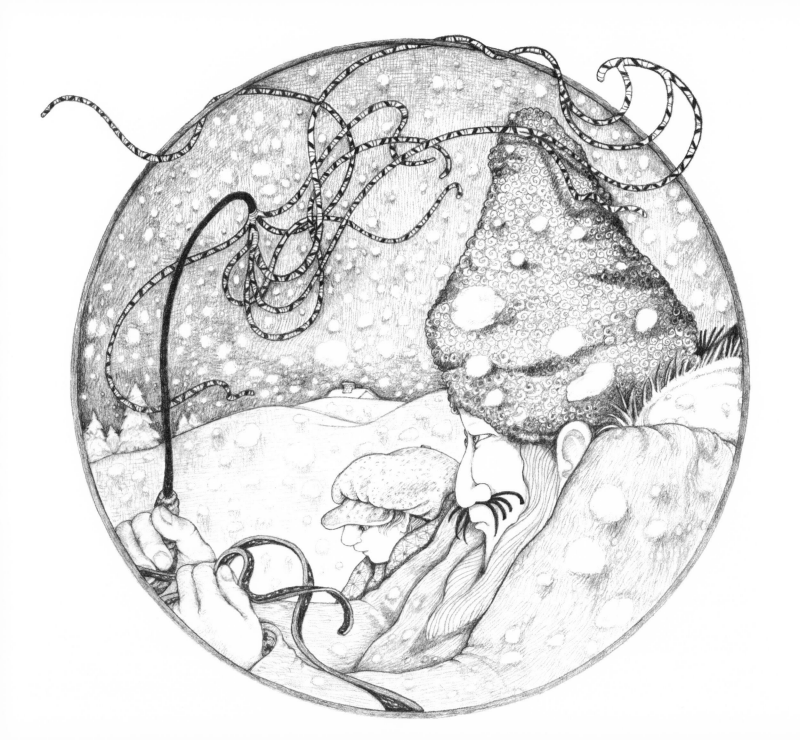

After his horse and cart disappeared down the road, Mama and Katya sat down for the evening meal. "We shall have one more egg from the good goose, Katya," Mama said cheerfully.

The child ate her soup slowly, thinking about Old Boris. He was hated in the countryside, for he would lend money to the peasant farmers at a very high interest rate and insist on collecting it even if the harvest was poor. When they could not pay, he took over their farms, which he sold to the large landowners.

"Do not worry, Katya," said Mama, as she looked across the table. "I have a plan for Old Boris. If it works, we shall keep our land." While the clock ticked softly and the firelight cast shadows on the walls, Mama told Katya what to do.

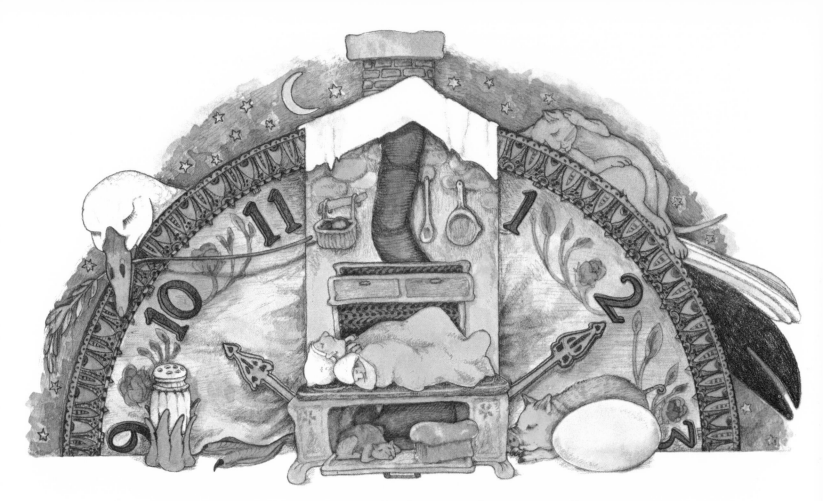

They went to sleep bundled in woolens atop the great
stove. The heat from the glowing coals warmed the little girl,
and she slept easily, knowing that her mother was a wise
woman.

The next morning Katya ate her bowl of baked cereal and put on a warm cloak. Mama tucked a small pie filled with meat and onions into her pocket and bade her good-bye. "Remember to repeat to Old Boris everything I told you. Especially to say, 'My mother sends her wisdom.' Do not forget his answer."

    With a fat white goose under each arm, Katya set off
through the forest. The trees were thick and the woods
were silent. She walked quickly, talking to the goose and
gander for company, for it was lonely. There was a smell
of snow in the air, and the wind moaned like a wolf crying
for the moon.

Soon the forest path grew wider, and she could see spires and roofs of the city houses through the trees. The streets were narrow and crowded. Men pushed carts along, and women cried their wares in the marketplace. "Come buy from me, good bread, good fowl, good brooms today." Katya stumbled along the cobblestones, wishing she were back in the forest again. The city seemed noisy.

An old woman showed her the way to the moneylender's house, which stood on a corner surrounded by a fence.

Katya managed to unlatch the gate and lifted the great brass doorknocker. A servant peered out and went to fetch his master. Soon Boris came to the door and opened it wide. Alexei stood behind him. "So you have brought my birds, and high time," snapped the old man.

"Yes, here are the geese for payment, and my mother sends her wisdom," said Katya in a quavering voice.

"Wisdom, is it?" said Old Boris with a laugh.

Katya's eyes were bright as she recited what her mother had taught her:

"Two well-kept geese, so I've been told,
May truly lay fine eggs of gold."

Boris shook his head and sneered. "What do I need with the wisdom of a peasant woman? Alexei, mark these geese in the book as payment, then take them to the market to sell."

Katya did not linger and started for home immediately. Without the geese to care for, the journey went quickly.

"And did Old Boris accept my wisdom?" asked Mama, as Katya took off her cloak.

"He laughed, Mama, and said he did not need the wisdom of a peasant woman. Then he ordered the goose and gander sold at the market."

"We shall see, we shall see," murmured Mama, as she warmed the child's feet before the stove.

The next month, on the day payment was due, Katya took two fat pigs through the forest to the moneylender. She kept them moving with her hooked stick, prodding them when they stopped to root in the rich, dark earth.

"Come pig, pig, pig. Come pig, pig, pig," she chanted, and soon they arrived in the city. The sun was high overhead when she reached the moneylender's house. This time Alexei opened the door, and his master shuffled out. "Here are two pigs for payment, and my mother sends her wisdom," said Katya, as the pigs snorted and rooted in the garden.

"What, your mother's wisdom again?" Boris asked scornfully. Katya drew a deep breath and spoke quickly:

"Five pink piglets, born anew,
Will squeal much more than old ones do."

The old man threw back his head and laughed. "If your mother were wise, she would not owe me money. It is the peasant who squeals, not the pig."

Katya did not answer, but turned and quickly went on her way. Soon she was back in the quiet forest, which seemed safer than the noisy, jostling city. When she returned home, she told her mother what Old Boris had answered.

"Good," said Mama, "all is going well, little one."

The festival of Easter was nearing, and together Katya and her mother decorated brightly colored eggs. Some were beet red while others glowed saffron yellow.

Before midnight of Easter eve, the Widow Petrovna and Katya went to pray at church. They lit candles and knelt inside the dark chapel while the stars in the spring night burned in the sky.

The next payment was due on the day after Easter, and Katya woke early that morning. As dawn streaked the Easter Monday sky and the cock crowed, Mama stood by the stove making breakfast.

"Today, Katya, you will take a good sack of wheat to Old Boris," Mama saïd. "It is heavy, so you must pull it in the little cart and take the dog with you for company."

They loaded the small cart with the wheat, and again Katya set off. She entered the forest with the cart behind her and the dog leaping ahead.

It was cool and the birds sang; bright patches of sunlight filtered through the leaves. The dog chased a rabbit, then returned and tugged at Katya's skirts to hurry her along. "I'm coming, I'm coming," she said with a laugh.

At high noon, she rapped on the moneylender's door and presented the grain. "Here is a sack of wheat for payment, and my mother sends her wisdom."

"What nonsense this time?" asked Old Boris, and Katya recited her mother's riddle:

"How is it that ten grains of wheat
Could give us all enough to eat?"

"I laugh at your mother's wisdom," snapped Old Boris. "She may keep it for herself. Alexei, mark the book for Widow Petrovna and take the wheat to market for sale."

Once more Katya went home and told her mother what the old man had said.

"Now we shall see who is the wiser, daughter," said her mother with a smile, and the two set to work in the garden.

The next month Katya did not visit the moneylender, and one day Old Boris and Alexei came to the cottage and knocked on the door. "You are late with your payment, Widow Petrovna," said the old man. "Do you have nothing to pay this month?"

Mama raised her eyebrows and spoke in a clear voice. "You must be mistaken, Old Boris, for my debt is paid off."

"Paid off, indeed! You still owe twenty rubles, either in money or in goods. Check the book, Alexei."

The boy turned the pages of the heavy book and read the figures. "Twenty rubles still owed, master."

The widow shook her head. "My debt is paid. The sack of wheat was the last payment, and you shall get nothing more. You must go to Judge Petruschka to ask for a hearing against me if you do not believe it, Boris."

"I shall, I shall," said the old man, nodding. "He will find that you are still owing, and I shall be forced to take your land in payment," and he drove off down the road in a cloud of dust.

Soon the day came when Judge Petruschka held court in the district. Old Boris and Alexei sat on one side of the room, while Katya and her mother sat on the other.

"What is the charge?" the judge asked quietly.

"This woman claims she has paid her debt, but she still owes me twenty rubles," said Boris.

"What has she paid you?" the judge asked.

"Two geese, which sold for six rubles. Two pigs, which brought ten rubles at market. A sack of wheat, which sold for four rubles."

"Is this true, Widow Petrovna?" the judge asked.

"No, your honor, it is only half true. My daughter will tell you what she offered Old Boris each time she took payment to him."

Katya stood before the judge and spoke out bravely. "When I took two geese, I offered him my mother's wisdom in this riddle:

> 'Two well-kept geese, so I've been told,
> May truly lay fine eggs of gold.'

"He did not accept my mother's wisdom. If he had, he would have kept the goose and gander, collected many eggs, raised a flock of goslings, and sold them at market for three times what he received.

"When I took the pigs to him, I offered him more of my mother's wisdom in this riddle:

'Five pink piglets, born anew,
Will squeal much more than old ones do.'

"If he had kept the pigs and raised a litter of five piglets, he could have sold them for twice as much as the two pigs brought.

"The third time I offered my mother's wisdom in this riddle:

'How is it that ten grains of wheat
Could give us all enough to eat?'

"He could have sold half the wheat for payment, planted the rest, and had a field of wheat next year, two fields after that, and four the following year."

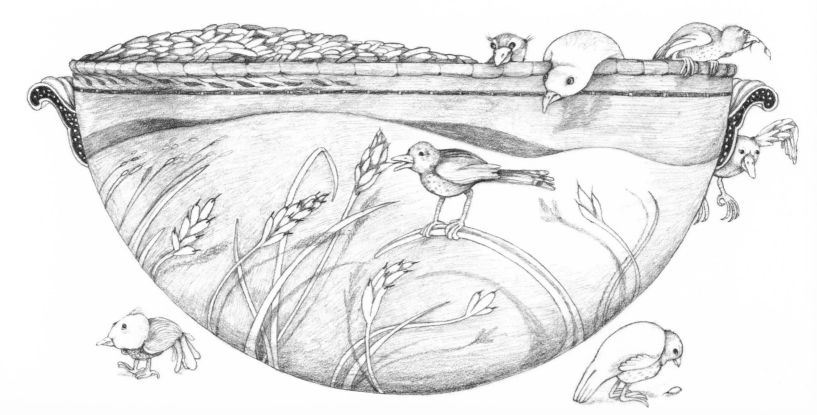

The judge looked thoughtful. "Is it true, Old Boris, this story the child tells?"

Boris glowered angrily. "Wisdom is not the same as money," he muttered.

The judge sat for a moment, scratching some figures in his book with a long pen. "Such wisdom," he said slowly, "is what feeds us all. I find, Old Boris, that Widow Petrovna has overpaid you some thirty rubles in her wisdom, so it is you who owe her money. I order you to pay her."

The judge would not be moved, though the old man flew into a rage. Finally he drew the money from his purse and flung it on the table.

Katya was trembling, but as she looked at the judge's face she thought she saw a tiny smile hiding around the corners of his mouth.

Soon all the countryside knew that Old Boris had been outdone by the wit of a peasant woman. Friends and relatives came to celebrate, bringing cream from their cows, flowers from their fields, and good strong tea to drink. "We share your joy, Widow Petrovna," they said. "May your land blossom with good fortune always."

ABOUT THE AUTHOR

After she obtained an undergraduate degree in English from George Washington University and an Ed.M. from Harvard, Louise McClenathan became a reading specialist for Fairfax County Schools in Virginia. While there, she contributed feature articles to the *Washington Star-News*, *Arlington Globe*, and *The Washington Post*, among other newspapers and journals. Currently she is Development Officer for Waynesburg College in Pennsylvania.

Deeply interested in family lore and legend, Louise McClenathan developed *My Mother Sends Her Wisdom* around an incident that actually occurred to the mother of a friend.

ABOUT THE ILLUSTRATOR

Rosekrans Hoffman was educated in her home state of Nebraska. After graduation from college, she assumed a variety of art-related jobs. A professional illustrator since 1973, she has six children's books to her credit, including her own *Anna Banana*.

Ms. Hoffman lives with her husband in West Haven, Connecticut.